This book belongs to

_____

CINDERELLA'S MAGIC ADVENTURE
Story adapted by JIM RAZZI

Bantam Books

TORONTO • NEW YORK • LONDON • SYDNEY • AUCKLAND

RL 2, 004–008

CINDERELLA'S MAGIC ADVENTURE

A Bantam Book/July 1985

*CHOOSE YOUR OWN ADVENTURE® is a registered
trademark of Bantam Books, Inc. Registered in U.S. Patent and
Trademark Office and elsewhere.*

*Concept: Edward Packard; Series Development:
R.A. Montgomery and Edward Packard*

Library of Congress Cataloging in Publication Data
Razzi, Jim.
   Cinderella's magic adventure.
   (Walt Disney choose your own adventure)
   Summary: The reader becomes involved with Cinderella, but
must make choices which will determine if she marries a
Prince or not.
   1. Plot-your-own stories. [1. Fairy tales. 2. Folklore.
3. Plot-your-own stories] I. Cinderella. II. Title. III. Series.
PZ8.R22Ci 1985   [398.2]   [E]   85-4026
ISBN 0-553-05404-X

Published simultaneously in the United States and Canada

*Bantam Books are published by Bantam Books, Inc. Its trade-
mark, consisting of the words "Bantam Books" and the portrayal
of a rooster, is Registered in U.S. Patent and Trademark Office
and in other countries. Marca Registrada. Bantam Books, Inc.,
666 Fifth Avenue, New York, New York 10103.*

PRINTED IN THE UNITED STATES OF AMERICA
DW   0 9 8 7 6 5 4 3 2 1

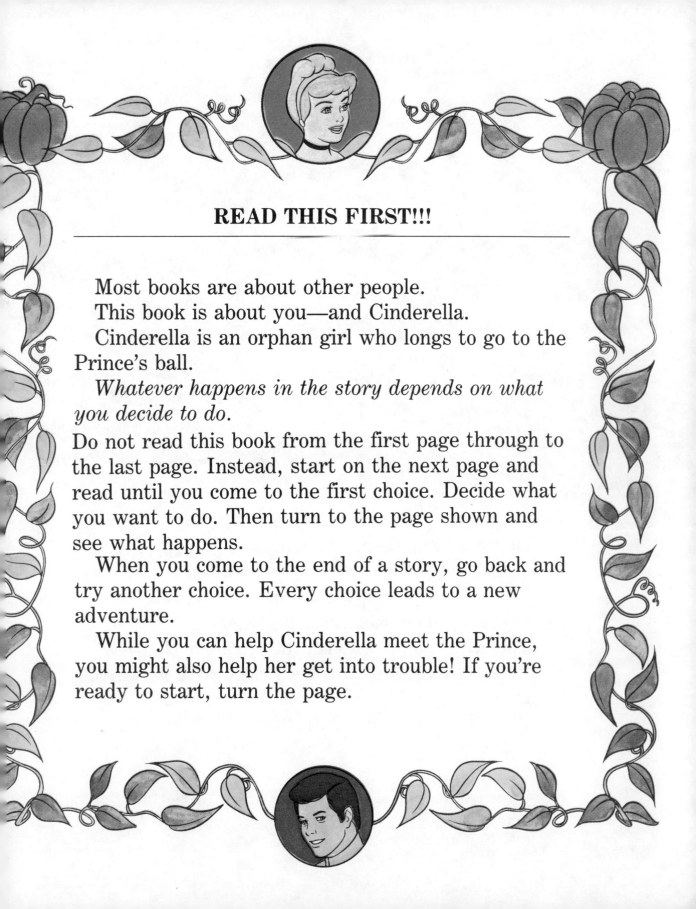

READ THIS FIRST!!!

Most books are about other people.

This book is about you—and Cinderella.

Cinderella is an orphan girl who longs to go to the Prince's ball.

Whatever happens in the story depends on what you decide to do.

Do not read this book from the first page through to the last page. Instead, start on the next page and read until you come to the first choice. Decide what you want to do. Then turn to the page shown and see what happens.

When you come to the end of a story, go back and try another choice. Every choice leads to a new adventure.

While you can help Cinderella meet the Prince, you might also help her get into trouble! If you're ready to start, turn the page.

In a cozy kingdom, nestled among deep forests and sparkling lakes, lives a handsome Prince.

The Prince is happy and kind and tries to do everything his father the King wishes.

The King's biggest wish, however, is that the Prince get married. But the Prince says he cannot marry until he falls in love with someone.

This gives the King an idea.

Go on to the next page.

The King decides to give a ball and invite all the young girls in the kingdom. Surely, he thinks, among all of them will be one girl the Prince can love!

You live in this little kingdom, and it so happens that *you* are invited to the ball. In fact, you are on your way right now, and you can hardly wait!

Turn to page 2.

As your coach moves smoothly through the night, you pass by a small garden.

To your surprise, you see a young girl in a tattered dress. She is sitting on a bench, crying. You stop the coach and run over to her.

"Why are you crying?" you ask.

"Because I can't go to the ball," she sobs.

Go on to the next page.

"My stepmother and stepsisters won't let me go."
The girl tells you her name is Cinderella.

You feel sorry for her. Maybe you could take her to the palace to see the dancers. Or maybe you could just stay awhile and try to cheer her up.

If you take Cinderella to the palace,
turn to page 4.

If you decide to try to cheer her up,
turn to page 6.

4   You help Cinderella into your coach and soon arrive at the palace.

But there are guards everywhere.

You look at Cinderella in her raggedy dress. They would never even let her *near* the ball!

"Let's wait here for now," you say. "When the guards aren't looking, we can sneak by them."

Go on to the next page.

You wait until the nearest guard turns his back. Then you and Cinderella dash into a large garden outside the ballroom.

"You can see the ball from here," you say.

You are just about to leave Cinderella, when a door from the ballroom opens and you see the Prince himself coming into the garden!

Turn to page 11.

You sit down next to Cinderella and try to think of something cheerful to say. But no sooner have you opened your mouth than—*poof!*—a little woman appears before your eyes!

"Who—who are you?" cries Cinderella.

"Why, your Fairy Godmother of course," answers the woman. "And I'm here to see that you go to the ball!"

Go on to the next page.

As you stare in wonder, Cinderella's Fairy
Godmother points to a nearby pumpkin patch.

"Quick!" she tells you. "Go get a nice fat pumpkin
and bring it here."

You run off to do as she asks, although you can't
imagine why she wants a pumpkin.

"And watch out for the Pumpkin Witch!" she calls
after you.

Pumpkin Witch? What is she talking about?

Turn to page 8.

When you get to the patch, you see some big pumpkins by a fence. And you see some better ones in the middle of the patch—right next to a scarecrow. But the scarecrow looks so frightening, you really don't want to go near it.

Should you pick a pumpkin by the fence or pick a better one near the scarecrow?

If you pick a pumpkin by the fence,
turn to page 12.

If you pick one near the scarecrow,
turn to page 16.

Suddenly you realize that the Prince might think
you and Cinderella are trying to sneak into the ball.
You wonder if you should hide somewhere.

But the Prince looks friendly. Maybe you should
just walk up to him and tell him Cinderella's story.

---

*If you decide to hide somewhere,
turn to page 20.*

*If you decide to talk to the Prince,
turn to page 22.*

12   You pick the fattest pumpkin you can find by the fence and hurry back with it.

Meanwhile, Cinderella has gathered four mice, a horse, and a dog. You put the pumpkin down next to them.

With a flourish, Cinderella's Fairy Godmother waves her magic wand . . .

Go on to the next page.

. . . and before your startled eyes, the pumpkin
changes into a grand coach!

The Fairy Godmother waves her wand again, and
the animals change into four dapple-gray horses, a
footman, and a handsome driver!

Cinderella's Fairy Godmother waves her wand
once more and Cinderella turns into a beautiful
Princess, with sparkling glass slippers on her feet!

Turn to page 14.

14   "Now you are ready for the ball!" says the Fairy Godmother.

"Oh, thank you!" cries Cinderella, looking down at her shimmering ball gown. "I feel so beautiful!"

"You are!" answers her Fairy Godmother. "But I must warn you—at midnight everything will turn back to what it was. You must make sure you leave the ball before then."

"I will," promises Cinderella.

Go on to the next page.

"Good," says her Fairy Godmother. "Now go and
enjoy yourselves."

Cinderella gets into her coach and it whisks her
away to the ball. You follow close behind in your
coach. It's going to be a wonderful night!

Turn to page 18.

16   You decide the scarecrow doesn't look *too* scary. You pick the nicest pumpkin you can find.

You are carrying it off when suddenly you hear, "Stop, thief!"

You turn around in surprise. An evil witch is standing where the scarecrow was!

"Steal my best pumpkin, will you?" she screams.

"I can explain," you begin.

Go on to the next page.

But the witch points a finger at you.
"You must be punished!" she cries.
Zap! Before you know what's happening, the witch has changed *you* into a scarecrow!
"Oh, no," you groan as you hang there. What a mistake you've made.
Your only hope is that Cinderella's Fairy Godmother will find you and break the spell.

The End

18   When you and Cinderella arrive at the ball, everyone is enchanted by her, especially the Prince. He asks her to dance. It seems he has fallen in love with her at first sight.

You go off on your own and have a wonderful time.

The evening flies by as Cinderella and the Prince dance every dance.

Go on to the next page.

Soon you see that it's close to midnight. Should you find Cinderella? Just then, however, someone asks you to dance again. You would love to!

But will you finish in time to remind Cinderella about her Fairy Godmother's warning? Maybe you should look for Cinderella instead.

___

If you look for Cinderella, turn to page 24.

If you decide to dance, turn to page 32.

"Quick, let's hide!" you cry, grabbing Cinderella's hand.

You and Cinderella run around a corner of the palace and into another garden.

There you find an old, unused well. The bottom is filled with straw, and a rope ladder is hanging down inside.

Should you climb down and hide in the well?

Go on to the next page.

Then you see a garden shed. That might be a
good place to hide, too.

All at once, you hear voices coming your way. It
sounds like the Palace Guard! You've got to make
up your mind right away!

Where should you hide, in the well or in the shed?

If you hide in the well, turn to page 28.

If you hide in the shed, turn to page 40.

22 You take a deep breath and walk over to the
Prince. He is surprised to find you in the garden,
but he listens closely to what you have to say.

When you are finished with your story, the Prince
looks at Cinderella.

Go on to the next page.

"I'm sorry your stepsisters were so mean to you," he says. "But even though you are in rags, your goodness and beauty shine through."

You sigh with happiness as you watch the Prince and Cinderella gazing at each other.

You are glad you decided to talk to the Prince!

The End

24   You decide you had better skip the dance. You look around the ballroom until you see Cinderella. You hurry over and remind her of her Fairy Godmother's warning. It's a good thing you do because she has forgotten all about it.

"I—I must go now," she tells the Prince.

But the Prince takes her hand and begs her to stay.

Just then, you see that it's almost midnight. You've got to do something!

Go on to the next page.

You ask the *Prince* to dance!

He is so surprised that he lets go of Cinderella's hand for a moment.

Cinderella runs out of the ballroom just as the clock begins striking midnight!

You dash after her, saying to the Prince, "I'm sorry. I didn't realize it was so late!"

Turn to page 26.

26   Cinderella runs down the palace steps with you close behind. You can see that her clothes are changing into rags again. And the coach has already changed back into a pumpkin!

"Wait!" you shout. "I'll take you home in my coach."

Go on to the next page.

You hear the Prince coming. "What's your name?"
he calls after Cinderella. But she doesn't answer.
She just runs faster. One of her glass slippers falls
off.

You stop for a moment. Should you pick it up or
keep on following Cinderella?

If you pick up the slipper,
turn to page 35.

If you keep on following Cinderella,
turn to page 37.

28   You scramble down the rope ladder into the well.
Cinderella follows you. But on the way down, the
ladder breaks! You and Cinderella land with a plop
on the straw-covered bottom.

Now you're stuck there—maybe for good!

Go on to the next page.

You look sadly at Cinderella.

"It's not your fault," she says. "You only did what you thought was best." But she looks wistfully at the opening far above your heads.

"How I wish we could have gone to the ball and danced with the Prince," she says dreamily.

You are just about to answer her, when—*poof!*

Turn to page 30.

30 You are at the ball, and Cinderella is all dressed up! And she's dancing with the Prince!

Suddenly you realize what has happened.

The old well must have been a *wishing* well, and Cinderella's wish has been granted!

How lucky it was that you decided to hide there.

The End

32   You smile at your partner and dance around the ballroom.

You have so much fun that you forget about the time. Then you hear the clock begin to strike midnight. With a gasp, you turn to look for Cinderella.

You see a crowd in the middle of the ballroom, and you rush over to see what's going on.

Go on to the next page.

When you get there, you see Cinderella standing in her rags!

"She's a fake!" someone in the crowd yells.

"She's not a Princess at all!" says another.

With a cry, Cinderella runs out of the ballroom. The Prince is so surprised, he doesn't even run after her. What a mess! If only you hadn't had that last dance!

The End

You stop to pick up the glass slipper.

But you don't notice that the Prince is right behind you. He stumbles over you, and you both go rolling down the palace steps as Cinderella runs off. You come to a bumpy stop at the base of a statue.

Turn to page 36.

CRASH! The statue falls to the ground and breaks into a hundred pieces!

"Oh, no!" cries the Prince. "That was my father's favorite!"

You shake with fear. You wonder what the King will do when he finds out that *you* broke his favorite statue!

Oh, why did you decide to pick up the slipper? If only *you* had a Fairy Godmother to get you out of this mess!

The End

You leave the slipper where it is. Finally you
catch up to Cinderella by your coach.
"Come, I'll take you home," you say.

In a little while, you are leaving Cinderella at her
home and preparing to go on to your own house.
"I'll come back in the morning," you say as you
wave goodbye to your new friend.
"I would like that," answers Cinderella.

Turn to page 38.

True to your word, the next day you tell your coachman to take you back to Cinderella's house.

But just as you arrive, you hear a scream from inside the house. You rush up to a window and peek in to see what's happening.

To your surprise, you see the Grand Duke trying a glass slipper on a grumpy-looking girl, probably one of the stepsisters. She is screeching in pain trying to fit into it.

Go on to the next page.

The Grand Duke sighs and shakes his head as he takes the slipper and prepares to leave.

"What's going on?" you ask the Duke as he is getting into his coach.

The Duke tells you that the Prince has found a glass slipper that belongs to a mystery girl at the ball. The Prince has fallen in love with her and has sent the Grand Duke to find the girl whom the slipper fits.

Turn to page 42.

You motion for Cinderella to follow you, and you tiptoe across the garden to the shed. It is full of garden tools, and you and Cinderella get very dirty as you look for something to duck behind.

You also make a lot of noise.

Suddenly the door opens, and two big palace guards stand before you!

Go on to the next page.

You are both so messy that the guards think you are just two ragamuffins!

You are marched off the palace grounds and told not to return.

You sigh. Too bad you decided to hide in the shed. What would have happened if you had hidden in the well?

The End

So far, the Grand Duke tells you, the slipper has fit no one. "Does any other maiden live here?" he asks.

"No!" cries the mean stepmother. She doesn't want him to know about Cinderella.

But you shout, "Yes!" and you run to find her.

Go on to the next page.

As soon as you find Cinderella, you rush her to the Grand Duke. He tries the glass slipper on her foot. It fits perfectly!

A few weeks later, you find yourself at a royal wedding. The Prince and Cinderella are getting married!

You beam with pleasure as you watch the happy couple. Everything is ending happily and all because of you!

The End